Billie Helps Robot, BeBop

By Bryan Carrier

Published by Pen It! Publications, LLC in the U.S.A.

812-371-4128 www.penitpublications.com

ISBN: 978-1-954004-99-3

Illustrated by Lizy J. Campbell

Dedication

I would like to thank the readers for purchasing, Billie Bop's Robot, BeBop. You may want to entertain your child with, Glasses for Wally.

I would like to thank my brothers, David and Tom for their support and encouragement. To Nigel for putting me back in the drivers seat. I am forever grateful.

To Lizy J Campbell and the PenIt! Publications team for their brilliant work with bringing BeBop to life.

Nine-year-old, Billie Bop is tinkering in the garage wearing a white lab coat with goggles shielding his face.

His friend, Ruby asks, "What are you building, Billie Bop?"

Billie Bop piles gears, rubber wheels, wires, electric motors, batteries, bottle caps, remotes, screw drivers and a drill on the floor next to two garbage cans.

"I'm building a robot!"

"A robot!" Ruby gasps. "Why are you building a robot?"

"To help with my chores. I'm going to teach him to cut the grass and take out the garbage," Billie Bop explains.

"Can I have one, too?" Ruby asks.

"We can build you a, Shebop," Billie Bop answers.

Together they begin building the robots.

Billie Bop attaches the wooden arms to the garbage can adding rubber wheels for the legs.

He attaches a bucket for the head.

"How does it work?" Ruby asks.

"I have small motors using remote controls,"
Billie Bop explains.

Billie Bop buries his head in the robots.

"Can we try them?" Ruby asks.

"Yes!"

Billie Bop flips the switch on the robots.

"Try Shebop, Ruby!"

Ruby operates her robot moving the arms up and down.

Billie Bop moves BeBop back and forth swiveling its head.

"They work, Billie Bop!"

Billie Bop starts the lawn mower.

"What are you doing," Ruby asks.

"I built him to help with my chores," said Billie Bop.

"Those are *your* chores, not his!"

BeBop cuts the lawn while Ruby is playing jump rope with Shebop.

"You should love him not work him," Ruby insists.

"He's a robot," Billie Bop said.

BeBop cuts the lawn faster and faster cutting through the flower bed.

"What's happening?" Ruby screams.

"He's out of control!"

Smoke begins to rise, sparks flicker, and BeBop
falls on its side.

"What happened?" Ruby asks.

"Not enough voltage."

"Not enough love!" Ruby huffs at her friend.

Billie Bop buries his head in BeBop's garbage can.

"All fixed," Billie Bop said.

"Are you going to play with us?"

"BeBop is going to take out the garbage."

"BeBop is your friend."

"I know," Billie Bop said.

"Start treating him as one," Ruby insists.

BeBop carries bags of garbage down the driveway. He sparks, smokes, tipping on its side spilling garbage on the driveway.

"Not enough voltage?" Ruby asks.

"Not enough love," Billie Bop smiles.

BeBop plays hopscotch with Ruby and Shebop. Billie Bop cuts the grass and cleans the garbage from the driveway.

"Want to play?"

"If BeBop will have me as a friend," Billie Bop said.

"Bop, bop," BeBop transmits through the remote.

"I think he said, yes," Ruby giggles.

BeBop and Shebop hold the jump rope for Ruby and Billie Bop.

"This is better than chores," BeBop transmits.

"It sure is," Billie Bop said.

"Let's all have fun!" BeBop transmits.

The End

 **Author Bryan Carrier** is a native of, Cleveland, Ohio who migrated to the warm sunny beaches of Clearwater, Florida in time to miss the snow flurries. He has an Associates degree in The Science of Graphic Arts Technology and Business. Bryan has worked in the graphic arts industry his entire career and is a Production Co-Ordinator in a busy printing facility. He enjoys writing children stories as well as screenplays. He has written pieces for the Vietnam Veteran's Memorial, Vietnam Women's Memorial, and Korean War Veteran's Memorial. He has also written a striking piece titled, Five More Minutes, for the Oklahoma City Bombing site. When he is not writing you can find him relaxing with his wife, Heather and their two dogs, Ruby and Bean.

CPSIA information can be obtained
at www.ICGtesting.com
Printed in the USA
BVHW021310201220
595534BV00011B/14